Bound by Attraction
Billionaire MF Romance Short Story
Author: Lilian Parrish

From the Author:
Thank you for purchasing this book.

Table of Contents

Bound by Attraction
Description

They met at a coffee shop. Lynn wasn't looking where she was going, Jude Lawson was just heading in. They didn't make eye contact, they literally bumped into each other, making Lynn spill her coffee on both of them.

And that wasn't the end of it. The next time they met, Lynn's car had broken down on the side of a deserted neighborhood. She hadn't expected to bump into him for the second time that day. And when he offered to help, she accepted because she didn't have any other choice.

For the next few days, as Lynn tries to find her footing, she stays a bit longer at Jude's place. Making it hard for both of them to ignore the attraction between them. But Lynn keeps her distance because she has had bad experience with men. But how long will she keep on resisting him?

Chapter 1

Lynn was getting her morning coffee as usual, a routine she had developed during her morning runs. She checked her phone as she waited for her drink.

The guy behind the counter handed her coffee and she mumbled a thank you, distracted by the numerous texts she was getting on her phone. The texts were from her overbearing mother, lecturing her on being responsible. She was 27, for God's sakes. She was a grown woman.

Suddenly she slammed into a hard surface spilling the coffee all over her clothes and shoes.

"Hey! Watch where you are going!" a grumpy voice said.

"You watch where you are going!" Lynn said before looking up to see a very tall man looking down at her. She had seen tall men in her life but this one was huge. He looked like the guys in wrestling matches. He could easily pick her up and toss her around like a rag doll.

This was not the day to anger another person, though. She quickly apologized while grabbing napkins to fix the mess that got on his white shirt. She wiped the front, trying to get some of the coffee out.

God, this was the hard surface and it was surprisingly pleasing to touch – no - wipe. She continued to wipe harder while looking at an outline of his chest that slowly appeared.

"Uhmm, you can stop now, it's okay. I got it," the giant said chuckling while taking the napkins from her hand. She blushed furiously realizing she had been assaulting his abs.

"Sorry," she said quickly as she ran out the coffee shop.

What the heck just happened? Her heart was beating so fast. She needed to get home and change. She was a mess.

She ran the rest of the way home pissed off at how she had reacted to her spilled coffee.

The tall guy should have bought her another drink. She ran till she reached the tall gates hesitant to go in. Her mother was really angry with her this time. She'd come home drunk last night, trashed the house, breaking her mom's treasured vases.

She had been acting out since she got fired about a month ago. It wasn't her fault that her boss was such a sleazebag, she had refused to sleep with him and exposed him and as a result, she got fired. Lynn had lost everything, her apartment, her savings; this forced her to move back in with her mother and step dad. She had worked so hard to move away from them but here she was staying with them until she figured things out.

She walked slowly through the back door into her mother's house, sorry, mansion. Elisa, her mom had moved in with her new husband, Mark after their wedding and got a mansion, lucky her. She could see her mom waiting for her by the door. She opened the door to reveal a very angry Elisa and a smirking Mark. She braced herself for the fight that was about to take place.

Chapter 2

Jude Lawson had a rough morning on his first week in this new town. He'd worked all week, and the one time he had gone out, some girl had ruined his outfit and assaulted him, not that he was complaining, it was entertaining to see her scramble to wipe the coffee out of his shirt and get distracted while at it. Too bad she had run out before he got her another drink. It was his fault of course; he had been too distracted with what to order for himself.

This town was the cliché suburbia. Everyone seemed happy and it was a good place for a fresh start. No one seemed to know who he was and that was a good thing. His last residence had been full of drama, from girls fighting over him, friends stealing from him... he just wanted some peace and quiet. He would start over again, make new friends and stay away from crazy women.

He hoped to make new friends, like the cute girl from the coffee shop. She looked out of place in this town and he had a feeling that she was more interesting than what he was used to.

He got to work, changing his shirt on the way. Good thing he always had an extra shirt for the nights he spent at his office. He had worked so hard to get what he had now; he wanted to enjoy it away from people who were always prying on him. His parents were opposed to him moving away, they had even found a girl for him pressuring him to marry her. He just had to get away.

Chapter 3

"Get out of my house!" Mark shouted. "Don't come back till you get your shit together!"

Lynn looked at her mum waiting for her to intervene. Mark had been shouting at her since she moved in with them. Her mom barely said a word and couldn't look at her.

"Mum? Are you going to let him kick me out?" Lynn asked with tears in her eyes.

"Lynn, I … you have to go," Elisa stuttered.

Lynn could not believe what she was hearing, her mother was letting Mark chase her out! She had nowhere to go. They had agreed to let her stay for at least a year but now Mark was letting her go and her mom supported him.

Lynn stomped to her room angrily, jammed whatever she could grab into her suitcase. She walked into the leaving room and saw her mother crying, being comforted by Mark and the sight of it only made her angrier making her slam the door on her way out.

She got into her car and started driving not knowing where to go, she had no friends here, no family, she was an only child and her relatives lived out of the country. Then all of a sudden her car stopped in the middle of the road, jerking her forward. She tried to start it, but it wouldn't start. She leaned her head back on her seat, counted to 10 then tried again. Nothing.

The tears she had been holding back finally fell. She couldn't breathe, so she got out of the car and sat on the hood of her car, her tears couldn't stop flowing. What would happen to her now, she was stuck. She had no friends, no relatives around, no money, she was basically stranded. She was crying so hard that she didn't notice the car stopping next to her.

"Are you okay?" a deep voice asked. Startled, Lynn tried to wipe away her tears and compose herself. She probably looked like a mess with makeup smeared all over her face.

"I'm fine," she sniffled as she looked at the guy.

"Coffee girl?" he asked recognizing her from that morning. Lynn's eyes widened at the absurd name and got ready to tell the guy off.

"We met at the coffee shop today, remember? You ruined my shirt," Jude said.

Lynn burst into tears again. Fuck! What had he said wrong? he got out of his car and walked towards her.

"Hey, I'm sorry, it was just a shirt, I got another one, you don't have to cry about it," he said. She was still crying.

Jude had never been in a situation where he had to comfort someone; he hugged her awkwardly while patting her head.

"I'm not a dog," she said after a while. He withdrew and looked at her; she looked so sad and puffy from crying.

"I've never been in this situation, what do I do?" he asked nervously. She looked at him with tears about to fall; he didn't want her to cry again.

"Let's go to the coffee shop and I'll get you that coffee that I made you spill and you can get anything you want," he said, leading her to his car, "We'll come back to your car later," he said seeing that she was in no condition to drive.

Lynn was wary of the giant guy and kept on sending him suspicious looks, but what did she have to lose, he was offering coffee to make up for the one he had spilled, she could even start solving her problems with a drink, besides, she had nowhere to go.

She got into his car and he drove towards the coffee shop, she looked at him and this is when she noticed how gorgeous he was and that was just his side profile.

He had a strong jaw line, luscious lips; he had a big nose, brown eyes which he kept on throwing toward her to see if she was still crying. He was a beautiful man. She has actually forgotten that she was crying as she kept on staring at him, she then noticed she had ruined his shirt with her make up.

The second shirt this day, this one seemed expensive and it really looked good on him. White was definitely his color.

He saw her staring. "Oh, I'm Jude. I'm not a serial killer if that's what going through your head." He chuckled.

She didn't say a word and continued staring. How was she going to pay for this expensive shirt? she thought.

"Okay, well, should I continue calling you coffee then?" he said chuckling. She quickly looked away embarrassed.

"It's Lynn," she said after a while.

"Pretty name," he said while looking at her.

The rest of the drive was quiet, when they got to the coffee house, she tried to fix her face as he looked at her.

Jude took off his shirt and handed it to her. "I don't have tissues here, and since you ruined it, use it," he said.

Lynn could not help but look at Jude's muscles. The man was built well and his biceps... oh lord. He was a very sexy man. He stretched to the back seat and took out another shirt which he quickly put over his head. Lynn was sad to see the glorious view gone, but she quickly wiped her face hoping that she had gotten everything.

They then walked into the coffee shop and she sat down while he ordered. He came back with her favorite coffee and donuts.

"How did you know?" she asked surprised, taking them with wide eyes from him.

"I asked the cashier what you had ordered in the morning in case you came back and I paid for it," he said.

That was so kind of him, Lynn thought as she delved into the donuts, She hadn't realized how hungry she was till she had eaten half of the donuts, she found Jude looking at her amused.

"What?" she asked.

"Nothing," he said with a smile on his face.

Even his smile was breath taking. He was perfect.

"Lynn, why were you crying?" he asked.

Her name sounded so good rolling from his tongue.

"I have nothing," she said on the verge of tears again. "I got kicked out of my house. I have no job, no money, so I guess I have every right to cry," she said bitterly.

"Come stay with me," he offered.

He was a stranger; she had gotten into his car without questioning him but going to stay with him? That was too much; she had watched many serial killer movies to set up herself like this.

"Before you say no, I won't do anything to you. You would be staying in my guest room and I'm barely home and it's till you figure things out," Jude said.

She looked like she was considering it but still cautious. She was really pretty.

"Okay, but I won't stay long, just a few weeks," she answered.

Chapter 4

Lynn could not believe that she had agreed to stay with a stranger but she had nowhere to go and this gorgeous man was offering her a place.

She hoped that she wouldn't come to regret it, but he seemed nice maybe it won't be too bad, he wasn't bad to look at every now and then. Plus she had made him pinky swear that he wasn't a serial killer, it was childish but she took pinky promises very seriously.

Jude wondered if he was crazy for asking her to stay with him but she looked so hopeless and cute. She was definitely attractive with her expressive eyes that lit up with every emotion and very kissable lips.

He wondered how it would feel to trace his tongue on her lips, feel the softness before kissing her. There was undeniable attraction between them but he pushed that aside. He did not have the time for such. Peace and quiet Jude he reminded himself.

They drove from the coffee shop to get her things from the car

"Give me your keys. I know a guy who can fix your car," Jude said after she had retrieved her bags.

Lynn handed him the keys and for a few seconds, their hands touched. He looked at her with those piercing brown eyes. Lynn felt chills down her back.

"Let's get going," he said clearing his throat. She let go quickly and got in the car.

"Where do you live?"

"Just around the corner," he said smiling at her. He had the perfect smile and teeth.

She was so mesmerized by how white his teeth were that she thought he was joking. Turns out, he wasn't, they approached a huge gate around the corner, not far from her mother's house.

"You live here?" she asked surprised.

"I just moved here," he answered while driving up the house. His driveway was gorgeous with what seemed to be a garden on the side.

The house was so big, bigger than Mark's, she thought.

"You really live here? I haven't seen you around."

"Yes, Lynn. I really live here," he said, chuckling.

The walked to the door and she wasn't prepared for the view before her, the house had high ceilings, white and grey walls with modern touches.

The hallway was empty except for a few empty vases, the living room was no different, having only a couch and a huge TV set. It was a typical bachelor's house but she didn't want to get ahead of herself maybe the girlfriend would decorate later when he'd settled.

"You live here alone?" she asked, following him to the couch.

"Yes Lynn, can I get you anything to drink? But let me warn you, I don't have a wide variety, there's bottled water and tap water, which one can I interest you in, m'lady?" he asked in a terrible British accent. This earned him a chuckle from her.

"No thanks, I'm okay," she answered.

"Well, let me show you around," he said, holding out his hand for her.

"You promise you are not a mafia boss or you don't sell drugs?" she asked, taking his hand.

"No, Lynn, I promise I'm not all that," he said laughing. She liked the sound of his laugh, it was deep and sincere.

"There's not a lot to see here, I haven't fully got to organizing and decorating yet," he said. No girlfriend - that made Lynn a bit happy. His hand felt so warm and nice. She didn't want to let go.

"There's the kitchen, nothing much there. I haven't done any shopping yet, living room, nothing special," he said, walking by to the staircase. She yawned unintentionally not realizing how tired she had been.

"Okay, let me show you to the guest room then you can freshen up while I get us something to eat. We'll continue with the tour later," he said leading her up the stairs.

The guest room was equivalent to her whole apartment; there was a huge bed, a night stand, closet and a bathroom

"My room is right up ahead on the left."

"I'll leave you to it," he said as he walked out of the room.

Lynn sat on the bed taking in the room, even the bed looked extravagant and soft. She lay on it thinking of how wild her day had been. She didn't feel herself dozing off.

Jude was in the kitchen trying to figure out what was edible and could make a meal. He resorted to ordering in; he hoped that she would like it. When the food came, he served it up and went to call her, he knocked on the door thrice but she wasn't answering.

He opened the door hoping that she was not naked, that would have been awkward and instead, he found her sprawled on the bed, snoring lightly. He chuckled to himself and walked out quietly not wanting to wake her up.

Chapter 5

Lynn woke up with a terrible headache, confused wondering where she was and that's when she remembered the deal she had made, groaning, she got up looking for something to stop her head from splitting into two, she walked to the bathroom hoping to find some pain killers in the cabinet. Unsuccessful, she walked to the kitchen to get some water, when she saw a note on the counter.

"Gone to work, will be back at 6, food in the fridge. Call the number on the fridge in case of anything."

She decided to explore first, try and figure out who this man was. She had nothing to do today, she couldn't go for her usual morning run in case she ran into her mother or worse, Mark.

Jude's house was bigger than her mom's, he even had a gym and movie theater, he was *rich* rich. She had to get her shit together; she wouldn't want to be named a gold digger. The kitchen cabinets were empty, she had to get some groceries and get some fresh air while at it.

She dialed the number, listening to the ring till a familiar deep voice answered.

"Yes." He sounded out of breath and in a hurry.

"Hi, Jude, its Lynn. So sorry for disturbing you, I wanted to know if you got someone to fix my car," she said.

"Oh Lynn, someone will bring it over in a few minutes."

He sounded so good over the phone; Lynn wondered what he was doing that got him out of breath.

"Do you need anything else?" he asked.

"No, I'm okay, thanks, bye," she said hurriedly and hung up.

She really needed to get laid. His voice was turning her on so much. She couldn't remember the last time she had sex. She had broken up with her ex a few years back and had vowed never to get into a relationship till she had everything she wanted. Her ex had been toxic, emotionally abusing her, always cheating on her, she had had enough and finally left he had tried to contact her a few times but she couldn't cave, not after what he put her through.

Maybe Jude was different, she thought to herself. *No, he's just helping me, I'll be out of here as soon as possible.* But he was so attractive and she couldn't deny the sexual tension between them.

She discarded her thoughts and went to freshen up. She'd have to go for some groceries. It's the least she could do for the man.

When she got out of the much needed shower, she got a text from Jude saying they her car was in the driveway. She dressed up and put on a cap and sunglasses as an attempt to disguise herself. The people in this town liked to gossip, news of her being around will have reached her mom before the end of the day.

She got into her car, which felt brand new. She would have to thank him somehow. She would cook her famous stir fry chicken.

She went to the grocery store, drove around for a bit trying to figure out her next move and when she drove back to Jude's place she found his car on the driveway. As she opened the door with the groceries, she found a stressed out Jude pacing around in the foyer.

"I thought you had left," he said a relieved look on his face.

"Went out to get some groceries," she answered finding it strange that he was concerned about her.

He helped carry them to the kitchen. He was still in his suit but the top buttons on his shirt were undone revealing a smooth, muscled surface. She couldn't help but sneak glances at him. He caught her looking at him and smirked.

"I'll cook. It's the least I can do to thank you," Lynn said while preparing her ingredients.

"I won't get in your way, I'll just go freshen up don't burn down my house," he said. She rolled her eyes and go to cooking.

The kitchen smelled heavenly when he came down a few minutes later, Lynn was standing with her back to him trying to reach utensils in the top cabinet. She looked so cute trying but she was too short to reach them. He got behind her and picked them for her. Lynn felt tiny, he was so tall. He smelled of mint and lavender, but the position there were in was compromising, her butt was pressed up on him. She almost fell trying to get out of that position.

He grabbed her waist to keep her steady, his hands felt cool on her waist, what a good day to wear a crop top, she thought to herself. He stepped away from her and set the utensils on the kitchen isle.

"What are you cooking? It smells good," he said.

"You'll love it! Here, taste it," she said, bringing the spoon to him; she scooped with her finger and held it out for him to taste.

His mouth was warm around her finger. He was looking at her while licking up her finger, those piercing brown eyes capturing hers and she couldn't look away. Lynn didn't think him tasting food would feel so good. She had offered it to him innocently but she wasn't complaining, he was doing a very good job. She felt faint, the whole thing was intense.

"It will be ready in a few minutes," she said clearing her throat.

She got back to stirring. He made her nervous.

"Jude, what exactly do you do for a living?" she asked while serving the food.

"Business," he said.

"What type of business Jude?" she asked. He liked the sound of his name from her mouth.

"It's nothing shady. Lynn, I have my own company. I create apps and games," he answered.

"This is so good," he added licking his lips.

Chapter 6

The rest of the week got them busy. Jude had meetings to attend to. Lynn was sending out job applications.

They saw each other every morning, texted each other during the day, mostly on what they wanted to eat, they are together while watching old sit coms and they had developed a routine which fit in their lives so perfectly.

The past few days, Lynn had learned so much about her roommate, he was very serious about his work, he loved gardening, he was some kind of billionaire, he had a sweet tooth and odd things he did such as changing his clothes throughout the day, he claimed that they were dirty, he was a clean freak, he ate ice cream with his teeth, like a psychopath. Living with him had been easy, he didn't come into her room and she respected his space.

The sexual tension between them was heightening each day. Lynn couldn't help but kept fantasizing how he was like in bed, probably a pro. He looked like the type that had many experiences. She had thought about kissing him; the man had this sexual energy that attracted Lynn to him. Maybe she would do something about it.

Jude had also been thinking about Lynn all day at work, she was interesting. He was extremely attracted to her. He liked how she reacted to him teasing her. He wondered how she would react with his dick buried deep inside her.

He got home excited to see her, she looked so sexy cooking. He wanted to have her so bad. He hugged her, feeling her body pressed up on him. He looked at her longingly, inching closer to her mouth. Not able to hold back any longer, he closed the small distance between them and kissed her tasting chocolate on her lips. She pressed herself closer to him.

He grabbed her and placed her on the kitchen counter while kissing her deeply, she moaned lightly in his mouth, this turned him on so much, he wanted her so bad, he had wanted her from the moment he saw her. She had her hands around his neck and was grinding on the counter wanting some friction to her aching center.

He tasted of a sweet wine they had just had. She wanted to feel the muscles beneath this shirt, she fumbled with the buttons of his shirt, giving up when she couldn't reach, she sighed and guided his hands to the rest of the buttons. Jude chuckled lightly as he took off his shirt.

"Bedroom?" he asked raising his eyebrows.

"Yes," she whispered out of breath.

He carried her with the legs wrapped around his legs to his bedroom. She didn't have time to look around, there were more urgent matters. He laid her on the bed, taking her sweatpants off; she had on a white lace panty that looked sexy on her curves.

"Mmmh, I like it," he said with a husky voice causing her to blush

He kissed her legs, trailing small kisses on her thighs, biting lightly leaving small marks. He then kissed her stomach going all the way to her chest. Lynn was breathing heavily, the sensations were heavenly, she had never felt anything like this before, he was teasing her and she wanted him on her, she moaned when he bit her underboob, sending waves of pleasure to her sex. She wanted him to touch her, relieve her of this torture. She pushed his head down hoping he'd get the sign

"What do you want, Lynn?" he asked.

"Touch me," she said in a small voice that she could hardly recognize as hers.

"Say it, Lynn," he said while looking at her. "I'm not touching you till you give me clear instructions."

Ugh, this is really frustrating. She had never been put on the spot like this before. She gathered what small courage she had before she whispered,

"Eat me out, Jude."

He immediately dove between her legs stretching them as far as they could go, pushed her panties to the side leaving her exposed. He looked at her with hunger in his eyes before he dove in between her thighs. Lynn moaned at the contact of his tongue with her pussy. His tongue felt warm and so good licking up her juices.

"Fuck, Lynn, you taste so good," he said. This turned Lynn on even more. She was moaning uncontrollably when he put his tongue inside her, the sensation was too much that she came on his tongue.

"Mmh, good girl," he said. His words made her pussy throb with need. He came up to kiss her making her taste herself on his tongue.

"Do you like how you taste on my tongue Lynn?" she could not even answer him as she managed a simple nod. He smiled at her and went ahead to take of his trousers. Lynn looked at him longingly, she wanted him so bad. She could feel her pussy juices flowing down her ass. He had on black boxer shorts which he took off to reveal his thick hard dick. Lynn swallowed, he was beautiful, she wanted to touch it, make him moan, but he had other plans in mind.

"Be patient Lynn, you'll get to touch me all you want later. Right now I have to have you or I'm going to explode," he said reaching for a condom on his night stand drawer.

He spread her legs wide open positioning himself in front of her.

He teased her a bit rubbing his dick against her wet folds. He loved watching her squirm in pleasure.

He pushed his dick inside her a bit earning an eye roll and a loud moan from her.

"Is this okay?" he asked.

"Deeper please," she answered. He felt so good inside her, she wanted more, she wanted to feel all of him. He was torturing her. Oh God, she had no idea sex could feel this good. He went in deeper as he cussed and moaned.

"I won't last long, Lynn, you feel so good," he said. She couldn't either, with each thrust she could feel herself getting close to the edge. She couldn't hold it anymore, she came as her walls contracted and relaxed on his dick, she thought she would die from the insane pleasure she was feeling. Jude came right after she did, moaning, his face twisted in a beautiful expression showing pleasure.

He slowly withdrew and went to the bathroom. He came out with a wet, warm towel and cleaned her up.

"You can use the bathroom if you want," Jude said.

Lynn was still recovering from the orgasm. She'd never had a man take care of her this way.

She went to the bathroom to pee and clean up. That was the best sex she'd ever had. She went back to the room and found Jude under the covers, he beckoned her to come over, she got under the covers. Jude held her and pulled her close to him, he smelled of mint and lavender. They held each other, as they drifted off to sleep.

Chapter 7

Lynn woke up to an empty space beside her; she remembered last night events making her blush furiously. The had fallen asleep together, she had expected him to be cold and sent her back to her room for the night but he had cuddled her all night, she had felt him leave very early, but sleep had taken over her. Jude had kissed her forehead before he left.

Lynn panicked a bit. What did this mean for their situation? Would it be awkward when they saw each other? She got out of bed grabbing the sheets with her, her clothes were nowhere to be seen. She saw a note on the night stand, next to it was a flower, a daisy. She smiled picking up the flower and smelling it.

"Gone to work, be back later. See you then."

Lynn felt butterflies in her stomach; he was the nicest man she had even been with. She looked around the bedroom since she didn't get a chance last night. His room was painted dark grey, there were some pictures of him when he was young at a football game, grinning at the camera with his front teeth missing, a picture of him with two people who she assumed were his parents, he had white sheets, she'd clean them later.

She walked to her room to clean up and figure out what she was going to do. She liked Jude but she did not want him thinking that she wanted him because of the money.

Jude couldn't stop thinking about Lynn at work, he couldn't concentrate on anything and often found himself zoning out. He had wanted to wake her up this morning for another round but she looked so peaceful sleeping. Last night had been the best night of his life, thinking about it made his dick hard, he couldn't wait to go home to her. He had left out a daisy for her; he hoped that he hadn't done too much. He found himself being affectionate towards her, something he rarely did.

He wanted to treat her good, give her anything she wanted, fuck her over and over again till they were both exhausted. He looked forward to the end of the day. He had canceled all his meetings. She had taken over his mind.

Lynn sent out more applications crossing her fingers to get something. She really wanted to get her life together, her mother had constantly reminded her through the numerous texts she had sent to her, Elisa had called to apologize to her but she couldn't come up with a reason as to why she had behaved that way towards her only child. Lynn strangely pitied her mother, she texted her telling her to meet her for lunch the next day; maybe they would find a common ground.

She glanced at the clock noticing time had gone by so fast, she was so nervous to see Jude. She didn't know what his reaction would be; they had to talk about last night. Lynn was in no position to get into any kind of relationship right now; she had to get her footing first. Last night had been the best night ever and as much as she wanted it to happen again, it couldn't. She had to focus and she did not need a distraction. Jude did not feel like a distraction and that scared her. This friendship that they had going on felt right and comfortable. The thought of telling him that it couldn't go any further hurt her.

The following day, Jude got in the house and found Lynn cooking. He loved this view of her. He enjoyed her food and always helped whenever she let him.

"Hi," he greeted walking to her. He hugged her from behind, getting a whiff of a lavender scent.

"Hi," she said turning to face him. The expression on her face was confusing to him. She looked so serious.

"We need to talk," she said avoiding his faze. His heart dropped. *What had he done wrong. Didn't she like what they had done?* he asked himself as he sat on the chair.

"What's up?" he asked trying to seem cool and collected. He was freaking out.

"About last night, it was amazing, Jude."

He let out a breath he hadn't noticed he was holding.

"But we can't do it again. I am not in that place in my life. I need to get a job and an apartment," she said sadly.

Jude didn't know what to say. It hurt a little to think that she didn't want him. But she made sense. He wanted to see her be successful but what they had last night was magical. One doesn't get that with just anyone.

He looked at her realizing that she was waiting for him to say something. He cleared his throat gathering his words

"Yeah, yeah, sure, it's okay, I understand," he said, faking a smile.

They were quiet, stealing occasional glances at each other. Jude wondered what she was thinking about. She was looking at him curiously. The energy in the room was awkward and tense.

"I'll clean up," they both said at the same time. This was part of their routine, cleaning up.

"We could do it how we do every day," said Jude.

They kept on bumping and accidentally touching each other. "How's job hunting going?" Jude asked in an attempt to break the tension.

"Good, I sent out more applications today," she answered. There was another long silence.

"I'm hoping for a response soon," she said.

"I'm seeing my mom tomorrow," Lynn said after a while. She had told him about the mother and step dad. He was surprised that she was going to meet her up.

"That's good," he answered.

"You know this doesn't have to be awkward. Let's pretend last night didn't happen," Lynn said.

"But it did happen. We just can't ignore that. Didn't you like it?" he asked drying his hands on the towel.

"I did, Jude, very much."

He was pinning her down with his gaze.

"You were amazing Lynn."

She looked into his eyes longingly. He looked even sexier now and she wanted to devour him. Fuck it, she thought to herself. She grabbed his shirt to pull him to her height; she lifted up on her tiptoes to reach his lips and kissed him.

Their lips moved together perfectly, none of them wanting to pull away even though they were out of breath. Jude pulled her closer to him as he kissed her deeper tasting her. He was surprised to hear himself moan into her mouth.

Chapter 8

"Jude," Lynn said while pulling away. He stepped back seeing the look on her face.

"Okay, we can do this, we can keep our hands off each other, we are adults," he rambled.

"We'll make it work, I promise," she said.

It was going to be tough seeing her and not touching her, he wanted her in his bed tonight. It felt right holding her as they slept.

He knew he wouldn't get much sleep that night. It was the same for Lynn who kept tossing and turning in her bed without an ounce of sleep. She had slept so well last night with Jude, sleeping alone would never be the same again. She wanted to be beside him.

She walked into the restaurant they had agreed on, seeing her mother seated at the furthest corner. Good thing she had not come with Mark. He followed her everywhere. She walked over to her noticing the annoyed face her mother was making at her. She was late, but only for a few minutes.

"Hi, mom," she greeted.

"You are late," Elisa said curtly.

What a great way to start a peaceful lunch, Lynn thought sarcastically. The waiter took their orders and there was an uncomfortable silence as they waiting for their food.

"Where are you staying?" her mom asked.

"Happy to see that you are concerned."

"Lynn," she said pleadingly.

"With a friend."

"Oh, which friend?" she asked.

"That's none of your business."

"I don't know what to say," Elisa said defeated.

The woman was unbelievable, how could she not have anything to say to the daughter she had kicked out with nothing?

"Saying sorry would be a good place to start," Lynn said.

"You know I have to do everything Mark says right now till he adds me to his will," she said holding Lynn's hand in hers. "A few more months, then you can move in back," she added.

Lynn then realized her mother was crazy. There was nothing she could do to fix their relationship right now.

"Bye mom," she said as she got up and left.

Jude wasn't having the best day either. He was unusually snappy and restless. He could not stop thinking about Lynn. He knew that her relationship with her mother was a rocky one. He hoped it had gone well.

He wasn't close to his parents. He preferred it that way and they were always nagging him about marriage and having a family of his own. They had even set him up with his ex-girlfriend who turned out to be after his money. Jude did not want to commit to anyone. He wanted to wait for what felt right.

He looked forward to going home to Lynn, even though they had agreed on being friends, she made his mood better

"Hi, how was your day," he greeted as soon as he got in the house.

"Good," she answered. He could see that she was sad. Lunch with her mother had probably not gone well.

"We will make it better," he said heading for the kitchen.

He brought some wine and two glasses.

"Thanks," she said while he poured her the wine.

"Do you want to talk about it?" he asked sitting next to her.

"No, thanks. She's not worth getting upset over."

Jude put on her favorite sit com and they sat together, laughing occasionally. Sitting with him in silence was never awkward. It was a comfortable silence.

They were feeling too lazy and tipsy to cook so they ordered pizza. They had gone through the bottle of wine now.

"This is a bad idea," said Jude as he went for the second bottle. He had to get up early for some meetings he had rescheduled.

"You are such a kill joy, bring that bottle over," said Lynn from the couch.

"Let's play a game, never have I ever," Lynn said.

"We are not 17, Lynn."

"Pleeaase," she pleaded looking at him innocently.

"Okay," he said defeated.

"I'll start, never have I ever shoplifted," Lynn said.

Jude took a sip. Lynn's eyes widened.

"I was 10. I stole lipstick for my girlfriend then, but she left me the next day," he said.

Lynn burst out laughing.

"My turn. Never have I ever worn matching clothes with my partner."

Lynn took a sip of her wine. Jude's eyes widened in laughter.

"Before you judge me, I was 16 and stupidly infatuated with the guy. We wore matching shirts to school and got matching tattoos later," Lynn said revealing the badly done tattoo that said queen.

"No way," Jude laughed as he looked at the tattoo. "This looks awful," he added.

Lynn was more fun when drunk. She had told him things she had never revealed to another soul. He had the most hilarious stories about his childhood. She could not stop laughing till her ribs hurt and she forgot the bad day she'd had.

Chapter 9

Lynn woke up feeling an arm around her. She tried to move it but the arm only held her closer. She gave up and opened her eyes to Jude's face. His mouth was slightly open and there was some drool on the corner of his mouth. She laughed at the sight and tried to move without waking him. Last night had been fun, the last thing she could remember was Jude daring her to eat a whole jar of peanut butter, looking at him now and he had brownish stains on his cheek and around his mouth. Had they kissed last night?

Jude grumbled in his sleep as he pulled her closer to him. She really had to use the bathroom but Jude wouldn't let her go, he kept on pulling her closer.

"Jude, let me go, I have to pee," she said, poking him on his chest.

Jude woke up startled.

"What?" he asked confused.

"I have to go to the bathroom and you are holding me hostage," she said. He quickly let her go assessing his surroundings. They had ended up cuddled on the couch. He had fallen asleep trying to carry her to her bed. He smiled remembering the silly things they had done. She had peanut butter all over her face. The jar was nowhere to be seen. They had made a huge mess.

What time was it? He had to get to work. He found his phone under the couch, he was already late and there were a number of calls from his secretary asking him where he was. He quickly texted her to reschedule his meeting again. He was in no mood to work, maybe he would get to spend the day with Lynn, nursing their hangover, although he did not get hangovers but it was a good excuse. He tried to clean up the mess.

"What happened to my face," Lynn asked poking her face into his room.

"Peanut butter," he answered laughing at her.

"Why is it on your mouth too? Did we?"

"No, you challenged me to a peanut butter eating competition," he answered. "Do you want to get something to eat? I'm off work today,"

"Sure," Lynn said avoiding looking at him taking of his shirt.

"Okay, see you in a few."

The restaurant they went to was a cute little place she'd never visited before. She had dressed casually not wanting to be too overdressed for brunch. It wasn't a date. They were just getting food together. She hoped she would not run into her mother or anyone she knew.

She was starving. She'd ordered almost half of the menu and everything looked great.

"I never knew you were such a good dancer," she teased. "I got a video of you last night, here look."

She showed him the video of him attempting to do a sexy dance. They could hear Lynn laughing in the background, cheering him on.

"Don't mock my skills," he said, smiling at her. "I could make a very good stripper!"

"Yeah, right," she replied, taking her phone.

She saw the notification of her email and she couldn't believe her eyes when he opened it.

"Jude," she yelled to him, her voice shaking.

"What?" he asked. She looked shocked.

"What Lynn?" he asked when she didn't answer. Her eyes were scanning quickly on the contents of her phone.

"I got a job!" she screamed.

He got up to hug her as they both jumped and cheered. People were probably looking at them funny but he didn't care. He was so happy for her.

"Let's get some drinks to celebrate," he said after he let her go.

"Yes, please," she said smiling. She looked so happy.

They finished their food and drinks and eventually went home.

"We have to celebrate properly tonight, at a fancy place, my treat. You deserve it Lynn," he said kissing her cheek.

Lynn was too excited to wonder if they were crossing boundaries by spending so much time together and whether this was a date.

Lynn had one - the only fancy dress she owned - a long black dress with a thigh high slit; she put on light make up. She hoped she wasn't too overdressed but she didn't care that much. This was her night, she deserved to look her best. Jude was waiting for her downstairs. He had told her to be ready by 7:30 and she was on time. She was excited to see where he would take her.

Chapter 10

Jude was waiting for her down stairs; he was on his phone about to call her again when he saw her. She looked gorgeous, the dress fitted her well showing off her curves and her hair was pulled into a loose bun, curls falling around her face. She was so beautiful that he almost forgot how to speak

"Ready?" she asked laughing at his reaction.

"Yeah, you look really nice," he said holding out his hand for her.

"Thanks, you don't look too bad yourself," she complimented him.

He walked her to the car, opened her door. "Such a gentleman," Lynn said getting into the car.

Jude could not stop staring at her. He stole glances at her when they were in traffic.

They got to the restaurant, Lynn had never been to such a fancy place, he felt so out of place but Jude was always making jokes and making her feel comfortable. He ordered some wine in fluent French. Of course the man knew French, he was perfect.

The food was nice and Jude kept on complementing her, making her feel all giddy inside. When they got home, she was too tired to watch anything and wanted to go to bed right away. Jude kissed her cheek, near her lips lingering there for a second. She pulled away blushed and went to bed. She could not stop smiling and went to bed thinking about him.

Lynn reported to work the next week. Jude offered to drive her there since it was close to his office. She was so excited to start her new job.

Her boss seemed so nice and she knew they would get along well. Jude had surprised her with flowers and coffee that morning. It was so sweet of him. Jude found himself doing nice things for her; he liked it when she was happy.

He insisted that they get lunch together.

This developed into a routine, going to work together, eating together. Lynn was finally getting to a point of fixing her life. She loved her job and she liked the routine with Jude even though sometimes she wondered what was going on between them. They would go on dates. He would buy her flowers and small gifts.

There was still a lot of sexual tension between them. Jude often kissed her cheek and forehead. She looked forward to those kisses.

She liked living with him but she still had to get her own place, she couldn't depend on him forever. Part of her did not want to move out, she had grown attached to Jude plus he always told her that he liked having her around.

Jude did not want to think about that now, but he dreaded the day that she would move out, he knew it was soon because she had told him that she had started to look for apartments. He did not want her to move out.

He felt great with her around and there was so much room for her in his house. He wanted to spend more time with her, maybe go on dates. He wanted her to be his girlfriend.

Lynn was getting into the house when she saw a car parked on the driveway, it wasn't Jude's and he had been out of town for some business. She walked over to the car inspecting it for the owner.

"Hi, is this Jude Lawson's place?" a chirpy voice asked. Lynn turned to find a gorgeous woman. "Yes, this is his place, but he's not around at the moment."

"I'm his girlfriend. I've been looking for him but his phone is off. When will he be back?" she asked.

"Girlfriend??" Lynn's heart dropped, he had never mentioned a girlfriend. The woman definitely looked like a billionaire's girlfriend. She was elegant.

"I have some great news for him," she said rubbing her belly.

She was pregnant? Lynn could not believe it.

He had lied to her. For God's sake, she had slept with him. A wave of emotions overcame her. She was angry and disgusted. That son of a bitch, she had even thought of them together in marriage.

"Could you help me out with his number?" the woman asked .

"Yeah, sure," Lynn replied giving out the number.

Cheating on a pregnant woman was so pathetic. She couldn't believe that she'd thought he was a nice guy. She felt so sorry for the woman.

"Okay, bye. I'll be back tomorrow," the woman said getting into her car.

Lynn watched her drive away, tears clouding her eyes. She had to get away. she couldn't be living with a guy with a baby momma while falling in love with him. She got in the house and packed her clothes in a hurry, she left him a note saying that she had moved out.

She drove to a motel out of town. She would get an apartment soon. She made sure to block him and all his social media accounts. She wanted nothing to do with such a man. She felt so heartbroken.

Why would he do lie to her? Did want to take advantage of her because she had nothing? She could not

stop thinking about the mess she had gotten herself into she
would focus on herself and get her life right.

Chapter 11

Jude came back home to a very quiet house, he called out for Lynn, he had been so excited to see her after being away for two days. He couldn't wait to show her what he had bought for her. He was finally going to confess his feelings and ask her to be his girlfriend.

He went to her room thinking that she was maybe taking a nap only to find an empty room, her clothes were gone. That was strange. He tried calling her but the calls kept on declining. He then saw the note on the kitchen counter.

"I moved out, thank you for everything. Your girlfriend came by."

Girlfriend? He had no girlfriend. She had moved out without telling him? Why would she do that and who was this girlfriend she was talking about?

There was a knock on the door. He opened expecting Lynn.

"What are you doing here?" he asked when he saw the person standing outside his door.

"Jude, I've missed you."

"What are you doing here, Sly?" he asked.

"I came to see you of course. Aren't you going to let me in?" Sly asked while forcing her way in.

Sly was his *ex*-girlfriend. She had lied to him just to get him to spend money on her. She's one of the reasons that Jude had moved here.

"I came by a few weeks ago but I found your maid," Sly replied, walking to the living room.

"I don't have a maid," Jude growled.

"Really? She was definitely dressed like one. She had long black hair."

"Lynn," he whispered to himself, "what do you want?" he asked.

"I'm pregnant, Jude, and you are the father. Didn't your maid tell you that? I told her the news and I assumed that she would tell you," she said rubbing her stomach.

"What? How?" Jude was at loss for words. His eyes widened as he realized what had happened. That's why she had moved out so abruptly. She had probably believed what Sly had said. He had to find her.

"Didn't you hear what I said? I'm pregnant, Jude," Sly shrieked when she noticed that he wasn't paying her attention.

"I heard you, get out of my house," he said angrily. This was not the first time Sly had told him she was pregnant. She had tricked him when they were together making him spend so much money taking care of her only to find out that it was a lie.

"Jude, I'm not lying this time. I am pregnant," she said.

"I heard you, Sly. Get out of my house and don't ever come back again," he said, opening the door for her. He knew she just wanted some money. There's no way she was pregnant. He hadn't slept with her for a whole year.

"Get out!" he shouted. All he could think about was how to get to Lynn. She must hate him.

"Out! Now!" he shouted when he noticed she wasn't budging.

"Okay, I'll go. You don't have to shout, but could I ask for a favor... I need some cash, Jude. I'll give it back soon."

He laughed and shut the door in her face. He had had enough of her tricks and shrilly voice.

He wanted to find Lynn as soon as possible. He did not want to lose her. He loved her.

Chapter 12

Jude paced on his living room thinking on how to reach Lynn; it was Saturday so she wouldn't be at work and he knew she could not have gone back to her mother's house and she had sworn never to go back. He had to wait till Monday in order to catch her at her workplace. He counted the hours to Monday. It was going to be torture waiting till then.

Lynn had found an apartment and she would move in the next week. She had been thinking about Jude since she left his house. He was probably picking names for his baby with his girlfriend.

Her heart ached at the thought. She had tried to distract herself but nothing was working. She had almost caved and unblocked him. She missed him so much but he had a family now. She had to think about herself.

When Monday morning came, Lynn was excited to go back to work, it was a good distraction.

Jude was so nervous. He had been in his car from five am in the morning waiting for Lynn to get to work. He could not go any longer without seeing her. He had to wait for four hours but that was nothing compared to what he had gone through over the weekend.

Lynn got to work early. She walked to her office only to find someone passed out in the doorway. She had been the first one to get there. The person was probably homeless looking for somewhere to sleep

"Sir, you can't sleep here," she said while trying to wake him up.

"Lynn?" a deep familiar voice said.

"Jude? What are you doing here?" Lynn asked, trying to help him up. Why was he here? He should have been home with his girlfriend.

He looked terrible, he had dark circles under his eyes and his clothes were shriveled up.

"Hi. You look so good," he said.

What a pig, she thought while crossing her arms and staring at him in disbelief.

"Shouldn't you be at home with your girlfriend?" she asked coldly.

"Lynn, please listen to me, I have no girlfriend, that was my ex. She still refers to me as her boyfriend but I have nothing to do with her. She's not pregnant. She wanted to trick me. It's not the first time she has done that. I don't want her, I want you."

"Bah!"

"I want *you,* Lynn. I've had feelings for you for a long time and I can't keep it to myself anymore. Will you be my girlfriend please?" he asked.

Lynn looked at him suspiciously. He could be lying but he looked so vulnerable and honest.

"No girlfriend, huh?"

"Zero," he answered quickly. "Except you, if you'll fill the role," he added.

"I'll have to think about it," she replied.

"It's okay, take your time," he said, sounding sad.

"I'll leave you to your work. Please unblock me," he said. "I won't send you more annoying videos."

"Okay, I'll let you know my decision soon," she laughed.

When Lynn got off work, she went directly to Jude's house. She had made him wait too long. She wanted to be with him and tell him how she felt. Before she could knock on the door a nervous Jude was standing before her.

"Yes, I want to be your girlfriend," she said. Jude grabbed her and kissed her before she could even react. She kissed him back, laughing in his mouth.

"I missed you so much," he said lifting her up. She wrapped her legs around him as they got into the house. Jude did not want to let her down. He wanted to hold her and kiss her.

She deepened the kiss using her tongue on him. They had both waited for this for so long. Lynn wanted him right away. They could talk later. She wanted to feel him inside her. She was grinding on him wanting to feel him on her.

They moved to the couch with her straddling him.

"Clothes off, now," she commanded him. He was surprised that she was taking control but he liked it, it made him more excited.

He got up took off his clothes leaving only his boxers on.

"I said take off all of your clothes, Jude," she murmured with a naughty glint in her eyes.

She wanted to tease him this time, make him beg.

The way that she was looking at Jude make him harder. She trailed her fingers from his chest to his dick, circling the tip, tasting the pre cum on her finger. Jude bit back a moan. She was so sexy.

Lynn touched his dick slowly at first, teasing him, circling her finger on the tip, she enjoyed watching him squirm under her touch. She went ahead to taste him with her tongue.

"Fuck Lynn," he cussed.

She took him in her mouth, whole sucking on his tip. He grabs her hair making her take him deeper. He moaned while thrusting his hips wanting to fuck her pretty face.

"Lynn, I want you right now," he said groaning.

He laid her on the couch undressing her, he was very impatient and he might have torn her clothes in the process. He needed her naked, she looked so perfect, laying there waiting for him. He grabbed her boobs squeezing hard; he sucked on her nipples and bit them lightly teasing her.

"Don't even think about it, Jude, I want you now," she said panting. He obeyed her positioning himself at her entrance, they both moaned when he thrust into her.

He moved deeper, harder inside her. She looked so beautiful begging him to make her cum.

"Cum with me Lynn," he said thrusting harder. That was it took for Lynn to explode, she was shaking with pleasure.

"You are so beautiful, I love you," Jude said while still buried inside her.

"I love you too Jude," she said smiling at him.

A few weeks after they decided to move in together. It felt like the best move especially since both seemed to function well when the other wasn't around.

"That's ugly Jude," Lynn said. "We can't have that in our house," she added. Jude pouted at her.

They had been furniture shopping for their new house which Jude bought without her knowledge. And so here they were, trying to buy stuff to decorate their house but Jude only seemed to pick all the ugly pieces. Good thing she had good taste.

They had been inseparable since they got together, it was the happiest he had ever been. He thanked God that he had stopped that day when he saw her crying on the hood of her car. He stared at her lovingly and kissed her on her cheek. She was his soulmate. He wasn't going to let her go.

He wanted her in his life forever. He was planning on how to propose to her soon. He wanted it to be special for her but for now he was just content being by her side.

"Should we get this?" she asked the man beside her looking lost in the furniture store.

God, she loved him.

THE END